The Angel

To my dearest Suzanne.

Beyond the Shadows

Tales that defy explanation

A hole appears in the fabric of our
imagination, the past manifests
Itself, seizing the chance to make
it their own, and just for a brief
moment the stage is theirs.

.

Contents:

The Angel.

5

The gate creaked loudly as it swung back revealing a narrow path leading along the side of the church wall. If it had been a gloomy afternoon, the wind rustling the trees over my head, I might have felt a little apprehensive as I entered the small churchyard that sloped gently down to the cliff and the sea that lay some two hundred feet below. But the sun was shining casting a warm glow upon the tall grave stones and the air was still; I could hear the distant sound of the sea gently breaking on the pebbles; the derisive laughter of seagulls; a blackbird sang brightly above my head.

The angel was much nearer the edge of the cliff than I remembered twenty years previously. Trees hung crazily over the edge their roots exposed like hands desperately clinging to life and hope. The intervening years of harsh winds and high tumultuous seas had taken their toll. I thought how I had sat on that hot July day, my back against a stone hedge, sketching joyfully every graceful line; the delicate angle of her neck and her hands raised in supplication towards the headstone; the wondrous beauty of her wings; I had struggled with her face for how can one recreate such sublime expression; the compassion in the heart of the stonemason who lovingly carved such beauty; his knowledge of the tragedy and the loss.

The hedge that I had leant against had long ago plunged into the sea; ten feet of short turf then the angel would follow suit; other headstones leant dangerously. It seemed that in this far corner of Norfolk no-one particularly cared, for had not houses gradually vanished, leaning crazily then breaking away to be swallowed up by the pounding surf? People had moved away leaving cottages to their inevitable fate; soon the church would follow suit. Some people said that perhaps it would be appropriate to let the whole cemetery slide into oblivion; a natural end; let the elements take back its own they said; for had not every flint and stone been worked and carved from the earth? The dead had already returned to the earth from whence they had come, so what could be a more fitting end?

Of course, this was unthinkable. The Victorian monuments would be rescued; the remains that lay beneath, re-interred in a woodland sanctuary safe from the hungry sea; there were complications; moving gravestones had legal implications; the cost was enormous and local hearts were weary. The young had shrugged their shoulders; the elderly too, facing the reality of their own mortality, raised their eyes to heaven at the very idea but despite it all this angel would be saved; this miracle of grace that had for so long knelt in silence; guarding faithfully the small child that had come to such an untimely end in the deep waters of the ocean; a child who I still believed, despite doubts over the years, had saved my own life.

A mist had risen that day; the day that I had drawn the angel. It had been hot; unusually hot for that part of the world where the sea breezes usually kept the temperature down. Bees buzzed lazily in the long grass among the wildflowers, drunk on an excess of honey; the birdsong so vibrant earlier had dwindled away. I had grown tired and drowsy by late afternoon, my pencil slipping from my fingers. How long I had slept I had no idea but I awoke with a start, the air cold and clammy, on my face, a white mist enveloping me. It was as if I had been drawn relentlessly under the sea; over the cliff by unseen hands. Kneeling, I searched for my pencils, pad, and rucksack, the mist now so thick that I could hardly see my own hands unless I held them up to my face. Then I grew still, listening my heart thumping. A whispering; like a breeze through the long grass of a summer meadow except this was no meadow and the air was still as death itself. I felt for my rucksack and rising, my heart beating uncomfortably, made my way along the line of tombstones touching each one, telling myself that soon I would come to a tall flint wall; from there to the door and the lane that ran down to the village. To my horror the whispering moved with me at my shoulder louder and more insistent now; names; Elizabeth Holden, Martha Granville, Winifred Grayson; pleading voices old and young; remember me, remember me they whispered; briars or something else which I dare not contemplate plucked at my coat. I began to panic, stumble; once or twice I dropped to my knees, found myself sobbing with fear, then I was lost; no flint wall just space and the sea loud in my ears below my feet. I stood still not daring to move, then dropping to my knees I stretched out my hand; there was nothing; an empty void in front of me and to my right; then, suddenly the voices ceased and soon there was gravel beneath my feet the flint wall brushing my right hand and then at last the door; had I imagined it - that small icy hand sliding into mine and leading me to safety; as I shut the door behind me I slid down by the wall my legs giving way and tried to gather my wits about me; the mist thinned and a silver moon broke through casting leafy shadows on the lane; many hours must have passed.

Next morning after an early breakfast at the village I had retraced my steps before returning to London. The sun shone brightly much as it did now, birds singing and strangely I felt no fear, the scene so beautiful and peaceful. My drawing pad lay as I had left it now slightly damp and curled at the edges. The drawing was much better than I had expected; the face was quite good after all; exceptionally good. Only later on closer study I realised that I could never myself have achieved such perfection.

From that moment my work improved, flourished; nothing presented any problems for me and my career took off and I was able to command huge sums.

Now it was my turn to repay the debt I owed to that small child drowned at sea so many years ago, leading me gently back to the land where his angel can continue to watch over him.

Tomorrow the work would start. A long campaign and a considerable sum of money, which I could well afford had convinced those in power, that the long dead were worth saving.

A new cometary had been prepared the other side of the village, next to the church which had been meticulously recreated, stone by stone, stained glass by stained glass and my angel will continue to stand guard over the small child that undoubtedly had led me to safety that evening so long ago.

NB. This story was born from an experience my wife and I had when walking the cliff near Ramsgate. A small church with a cemetery attracted us as cemeteries are wont to do and we opened the small iron gate and browsed among the tombstones admiring the occasional angel.

Then we both noticed an elderly figure dressed in rather old fashioned black clothes and a bonnet, the dress brushing the long grass. For a moment we were distracted by a particular beautiful angel, then I looked again and there was nothing to be seen. Of course, there are many explanations but it left a doubt in my mind and a story in my head!

Molly Parish.

11

I had, in 1918, like many others, emerged from a war, where all aspects of reality, whatever we assume to be reality, that is, had ceased to exist. The Great War has been chronicled so many times, individuals experiences, related and documented, it could be thought that there was little that could be added. Anyone who had taken part and survived the death and destruction, during those years, could tell tales of lost souls, in the fields of the Somme, the mud of Flanders and Passchendaele: dim figures, forever seeking a way back home.

So fifty years later, when as a seventy year old lighthouse keeper, leaving the Bay Rock Tower off the Cornish coast, for the last time, with two of the assistant keepers, I was not surprised to see the slim figure of Molly Parish, standing out on the gallery, her hand raised in farewell. My companions were looking back too, with, do doubt, mixed feelings, but I knew that they could not see Molly. On and off, for the last forty years, Molly had been a companion, on lonely nights, on watch. I raised my hand to her.

'Yes, goodbye,' Matthew Dark, my second in command, said, seeing my arm raised. 'Thank God Trinity has come to its senses. It's no life for a young man, anymore.'

I smiled sadly. 'I will miss her,' I said, my words unheard whipped away by the wind.

Tonight the light would come on automatically, controlled from the shore, the first of the lighthouses to go automatic. Molly Parish would sit alone, or wander, seeking, seeking, as she had since 1888, when, as the only survivor of a Packet from America, bound for Plymouth, that, despite the Bay Rock light, had run aground on the rocks, as, like a moth to a candle, it had been drawn, helplessly to the light, pushed on by forty foot waves.

Molly Parish had been pulled ashore, an eighteen year old bride, but had died soon after, in the arms of the keeper Josiah Wedge.

After the war, Trinity House, were asking for apprentice lighthouse keepers. The more I thought of it, the more I realised that it was what I had been seeking; a life of peace and quiet, cut off from the demands and complications of life on shore, after the horrors that I had witnessed on the Western Front.

Over the next few years I was sent to lighthouses all over the country, some miles offshore, others on land, and it was on the Bay Rock, where I was promoted to head keeper, that I first saw Molly Parish. Whether it was something in me that conjured her up in the darkness of the tower, or whether other keepers had seen her before and were too afraid to talk about it, I will never know.

Lighthouses lend themselves to rumours of hauntings by their very nature; the loneliness of men during the two long months on duty, the long hours, of isolation during which, the mind escapes the boundaries of reality. The tiredness that sets in, from the very nature of their work, and the longing for leave and connection with their loved ones again on the mainland. Then there is the sea. The constant rise and fall; the savagery and uncaring nature of the storms, the wind howling through nooks and crannies and the very tower itself shaking as rocks are rolled against its base. It is not a life for everyone, but it suited me and my life on the rock was infinitely better than my life ashore, where I had not made any family ties.

Bay Rock Tower was one of the tallest of the offshore lighthouses, only the Eddystone and The Bishop, higher. Twelve miles off the coast out in the Atlantic, it had ten floors, the lowest being the store and then the water and fuel floors, before the iron door opened on to the set off, the lower balcony, sixty foot above the rock, with irons rungs leading up from the rock. A central iron tube held the chain and weights that had to be hauled up every hour, to keep the lantern revolving, and was buried deep into the rocks below. A narrow iron staircase wound up the inside walls.

A boat could not get close enough for a man to cross over, even in the mildest weather. A bosuns chair, winched onto the set off, was the only way, and in storms with the waves rising and falling forty feet, it was a hazardous and terrifying operation.

Inside it was naturally dark, dimly lit by paraffin lamps that flickered with the constantly moving air, for however strongly built with walls four foot, thick the wind found a way through sometimes creating a high whining sound. All these things one got used to and almost missed when walking on the foreshore. I had a cottage facing the sea, the end of four terraced owned by and maintained by Trinity House. As an unmarried man I had the smallest, even though my status as head keeper would have demanded the largest.

So what of Molly? I first saw her in the lantern room, while tending the lights. My assistant keeper, Richard Lobb, was just coming of duty and was on his way down to make a cup of tea, before retiring to bed in the small banana cupboards that bordered the walls of the bedroom; banana because it was impossible to lie straight.

She was standing looking out to sea, a small slim figure, dressed in black, tightly fitted waist and her dress brushing the floor. A bonnet on her head, tied underneath her chin with black ribbon, a glimpse of black curls peeping from underneath. For a moment I was speechless, in shock, so much so that Richard turned and asked me if I was alright. It was then that I realised that only I could see her. Then she turned and smiled, before vanishing. Sometimes she would be gone for weeks and then she would appear for several days in succession. One bright day, while I was out on the balcony reading, I glanced down at my feet and the name Molly Parish was spelt out in tiny shells, so that's how it was that I knew her name and was able to connect her with that shipwreck of the 'Eastern Star' in 1888. Some nights she was more distinct, almost solid as if you could hold her, touch her lips, caress her hair. I looked forward to my night shifts, sometimes even swapping the day shift so that I might sit peacefully with her. It sounds madness and whether the madness was inside my head I will never know. She never spoke, but indicated that she was listening to my words. Lighthouse Keepers are renowned for talking to themselves so my behaviour was not seen as strange. Over the years I began to understand that her absences, coincided with disasters at sea, and it was only when the sea was kind that she was able to be with me.

As I reached the age of retirement which coincided with the automation of the light, I asked her to come with me. Of course it was a foolish request by a foolish old man.

The keepers houses were to be converted to holiday homes and Trinity offered alternative accommodation for us in the town but I knew that I could not settle between four square walls. I'd had my eye on a broken down rusty old trawler, that was laying up on the River Tavy, just off the Tamer. It was in generally good condition on a good mooring. It suited me to a tee and had a little garden with the mooring. I aimed to spend out the last of my days there.

Molly Parish is still with me to this day; that eighteen year old bride. Sometimes she goes off for weeks on end, but always returns. I believe that she seeks her husband among the waves on Bay Rock. Perhaps one day she will find him and be at rest. I often visit her grave, in the little village of Tordene, a small cemetery overlooking the sea, finding such comfort in my old age, sitting on a seat that I have had erected under an ancient oak. Sometimes she is by my side, so near yet so far.

It is possible on a clear day, to see the Bay Light. At night it sends out its beam every ten seconds, a stream of silver across the water, touching her headstone.

Molly Parish Born 6th June 1870.
Died 19th November 188
Sole survivor of the Eastern Star
wrecked on the Bay Rock, 18th November 1888
She lies now at peace
In the arms of our Lord

The Visitor

A loud knock on the door brought me to my senses.

I had been dozing in front of the roaring fire, finding myself reading over and over the same words on the page of my book. It had slid to the floor at my feet.

For a moment I thought that I must have imagined it, for the snow now lay thick on the ground and the road from across the moor from Tavistock must be impassable. I was not worried, for I had everything in that I needed, to tide me over Christmas and beyond.

I had grown used to the weather that Dartmoor had to offer, during my previous stays at my cottage. Previous to my arrival from London, I had telegraphed Mrs Hughes in the village and arranged a delivery of Christmas fare. On my arrival I had been pleased to see, not only a fire welcoming me, but my fridge well stocked with turkey and other delights. A note had been left by Mrs Hughes, informing me that she would be up in the morning to cook my breakfast and prepare Christmas dinner. Mrs Hughes, the post mistress, a widow, was an excellent cook and had served me well over the last ten years, when I had the good fortune to purchase the cottage as a retreat from the smoke and noise of the City.

I had arrived that afternoon on the train from Paddington to Plymouth, then by Stagecoach, that conveniently met up with the train. I was a great lover of timetables and often planned trips linking trains and coaches to far distant parts and was rarely disappointed in the accuracy they displayed.

The snow had begun to settle, when I had mounted the Stage, the Coachman and his postillion were anxious to be off. To my surprise the coach was empty. As we rattled along the road, climbing the hill onto Dartmoor, the church and the prison at Princetown, barely discernible in the fading light, the snow building up on the windows, I had been overtaken with a strange feeling of loneliness that seeped through my whole being, and I began to long for the familiar fireside and comfort of my cottage.

An old ballad came to mind, that I had recently heard sung in a public house off Cheapside, concerning the devil forcing the Coachman to drive him to Hell, and his eventual escape, from the hands of the evil one. I had drunk a little too much brandy at the Station Inn and my imagination ran riot in the cold and empty carriage. I was thankful, when the Coachman pulled the horses to a halt with much shouting, opposite my cottage on the outskirts of the village; thankful that the gates of hell were not beckoning, only my picket gate now topped with snow, as I stepped down and took my luggage from the postillion.

The coachman shouted his farewell and the two huge black horses sprang into action their breath fiery on the icy air, their hooves slipping on the freezing snow. I watched the lights fade into the distance, then pushing my gate open, I had trod the soft snow to warmth and safety.

There it was again. A knock. Louder this time, jolting me into action, the warmth of the fire exchanged for the cold of the hall, the paraffin lamp in my hand, breaking up the dark shadows on the paintings that lined the walls.

To my surprise a young woman stood on the doorstep, her cloak and hood, covered in snow, her red hair escaping upon her cheeks, her eyes wide with fear.

Sensing her need for sanctuary, I stepped aside and she passed me, her cloak brushing against me and was warming her hands by the fire by the time I returned. I poured a brandy and placed it in between her cold hands.

'You must be frozen,' I managed, for want of anything more sensible to say. For a moment it was as if I had been waiting for her. As if I had waited all my life.

'I am,' she whispered. 'Thank you.'

It was then I noticed her condition. Her cloak had fallen open. She was with child.

My first thought was to summon Mrs Hughes from the village; it was, as if she had read my thoughts.

'Can I rely on your discretion, sir,' she said, lifting her face to me. She was indeed beautiful, softly and well spoken. No village maiden in trouble.

I hesitated for a moment. I was used to being asked for my discretion in such matters, for I had been serving as a solicitor for some years in the City.

'If you wish. Here, let me take your cloak,' I said.

'No sir, thank you. I will warm myself and be on my way. I have to reach Tavistock by morning.'

'You cannot possibly go out in this again,' I protested. 'Besides your - .' I hesitated.

'My condition? That is the very reason, sir,' she whispered.

'Stay there by the fire. I will get you something warm; a bowl of hot stew. I am no cook,' I laughed, trying to ease the situation. 'My friend in the village has prepared such a dish and I only have to heat it up. We will decide what to do when you have recovered.'

I searched everywhere for her when I returned with a bowl of steaming hot stew, but she was nowhere to be seen and the snow had already covered her footprints on the path, if they were ever there at all. Had I had imagined the whole thing? Too much brandy; the strange ghostly ride in the Stage. I returned to my fireside, my head buzzing. There on the rug lay a spotless handkerchief. I picked it up and examined the prettily embroidered blue forget-me-nots, the initials GH.

I never mentioned my strange experience for fear of being ridiculed. It was only a few weeks later, that by chance, when researching the history of a client in the archives of the City Library, I came across a report of how a young woman, Lady Georgina Halstock, had been found dead on the outskirts of Tavistock, during a snowstorm in 1856.

At the inquest it had been said that she was with child by a gardener who worked on her estate, and had fled from the fury of her husband. A woman from our village had given evidence how the woman had knocked on her door appealing for shelter, but noting her condition, she had turned her away.

The magistrate had been quite severe in his summing up. saying that, although the nature and cause of the deceased's condition was one of utter shame, much could be said for helping a fellow human being in such circumstances and avoiding such a tragedy.

I had kept the handkerchief in the hope that I might see her again one day, for she had stirred my heart in no uncertain manner. A foolish bachelors romantic notion, no doubt.

In my rooms, that evening, I could not stop thinking about her, trying to conjure up her pale cheeks, her wide green eyes. Her hood had fallen back for moment, that evening and her hair was the colour of the sunset low over the sea.

I felt a strong need to hold that handkerchief in my hand again but search and search, as I did that night and some days beyond, there was no sign of it. I am a meticulous man as my profession requires, but I have no explanation as to its disappearance other than that it was never there in the first place and purely my imagination.

In the years that followed, when escaping from the City, I listened for that knock, but it never came, and my hope of it coming faded with the years. Mrs Hughes died. I sold the cottage to a young couple and retired to the seaside at Sidmouth, where I would sit and watch the sun dropping low over the sea, hearing, sometimes, her gentle voice, the words lost on the wind. The strange thing was that the loneliness that had plagued my life up until that night, never returned. The touch of her cloak brushing against me, her beauty and the gentleness of her voice remained with me, enfolding me like a protective blanket.

The House Near Zennor.

24

For anyone that doesn't know Cornwall, Zennor is a small village about six miles from Penzance. Head west for about two miles and my house stands looking out to sea. The day that I first set eyes on it, the sun was high in the sky, the sea blue, a small sandy bay lay at the bottom of the cliff. The house itself stood stark, uncompromising grey granite, four windows and a door like in one of those children's paintings. Next door, a Wesleyan chapel nestled into a small copse of windblown and tortured trees, holding almost desperately onto a number of gravestones leaning away from the cliffs edge, their words and dates barely distinguishable.

The house inside was bare of any comfort as might be expected, for I had been informed that it had been empty for five years. A white ceramic sink and wooden draining board, an old kitchen range with a metal chimney, the door into the living room sporting four rusty hooks; the floor black and red quarries.

The rest of the house, the living room and two bedrooms upstairs was no better, except for wide pitch pine floorboards that I was told, would have been rescued off the beach, the remains of ancient shipwrecks.

Was this house built with love? In 1756 one could imagine a couple planning their life together, the granite being dressed at the quarry in Newmill, just a couple of miles away, and transported by cart, the walls gradually growing out of the ground, the excitement mounting. Or am I being over romantic?

Can a house be evil? Not to start with, I feel, as it stands new and proud ready for whatever is thrown at it, gales, snow, rain and, in this case, the salt spray from the sea. But as the years unfold it takes on the characteristics of its occupants as they come and go, their births and deaths, good and bad. Elements that are drawn into the very fabric of the stones, and lie waiting to emerge when the time is right.

And so it was with me. The time was right and the house gradually came alive, responding to my despair, the despair that I had hoped to escape from after the war, leaving London and a broken marriage. I had hoped to settle quietly, keep myself to myself and write, putting my whole past behind me, but of course I brought it with me. One's past is an umbilical cord that cannot be broken; it trails behind you like a shadow, as you face the sun hoping for resolution but finding none.

I had fought right through the war from the Somme to Passchendaele, where I had been wounded and invalided out. I still had a slight limp, but my wounds ran far deeper than that. Years of mud, lice and rats, gunfire, death and destruction had left its mark, and returning to a wife who had difficulty in imagining such utter desecration, and parents who thought me a hero, especially my father, led me to consider a way out. Having decided that I had not the courage to end my life, I consulted a doctor, a friend who I had become acquainted with at Cambridge back in 1912. He, advised me to seek peace, to retreat to Cornwall, where I had spent many happy weeks as a boy, and write. so here I was on a sunny day in July 1919, picking my way around the garden, the house and the churchyard, while I waited for the agent who was travelling from Penzance.

I myself was staying in a lodging house in St Ives. I had hired a horse and ridden the six miles. My spirits had lifted as each mile unfolded, the sea on my right, the path dropping steeply and rising, sheep scattering under our feet, the wind and sea air on my face. The despair that had dogged me for months lifted and I felt newly born, if that is not an exaggeration.

Having decided to go ahead with the purchase, which was well within my means, and obtained advice on a local builder to approach, the agent seemed reluctant to stay longer than necessary and wishing me well, set off back to Penzance. He seemed to know very little of the history of the house, suggesting that I might gain information from the deeds, or the archives in Penzance Town Hall.

It was late afternoon by the time he left and a mist was rising off the sea. The coast path back to St Ives came very near the edge of the cliff at times and I began to see that the journey could be one of danger, so I decided to seek a bed for the night in the nearby village of Morvah, and stabling for my horse. Luckily, I had hired the horse for a week and informed my landlady that I might spend a couple of days or so exploring the coast, so I had no worry as to being missed.

As I rode past the chapel, I glanced into the churchyard and was astonished to see a figure in black, a youngish woman, I presumed, standing at a gravestone, her back to me. I hesitated, then rode on, not wishing to disturb her, but she remained with me through that night and the following days, that slim figure in mourning, and it was some time before I saw her again in very different circumstances, which I would rather forget, if I was able.

My house was gradually put into shape and became moderately comfortable with new furniture bought in Penzance. The lodging I found at Morvah was so comfortable that I stayed on, visiting the house now and then to check on progress, while exploring the area on foot, my horse having been returned to the livery stables from whence it came. I determined to purchase a livelier steed when I had settled.

I walked one day to St Just, marvelling at the rugged beauty of the coast and the engine houses that stood on the very edges of the rocks as if any moment they might fall into the sea. Coming back, the light fading, I met streams of miners changing shifts, near Pendeen and Bottalock; some wearily touched their caps to me; others met my smiles with hostility, for which I could hardly blame them, being a gentleman of leisure, while they laid down their lives for such miserable recompense.

One morning after visiting the house, out of curiosity, I sought the gravestone where the young woman had stood.

It was quite old, covered in lichen like many of the others; a curved top, an angel carved above the inscription. I was loath to scrape away the lichen, out of respect to the young woman, who most certainly, in my mind, would be visiting again. I could just make out a date, 1848. Then I noticed a red rose at the foot of the stone, not quite fresh, it's petals wilting. I had not noticed it before, as a thick carpet of wet autumn leaves had begun to cover the ground over the last few days, with the strong westerly winds.

The name on the gravestone was Nancy Trevarrick, 1848 – 1858, beloved daughter of Thirza and John Trevarrick of this Parish.

That evening I mentioned the gravestone to my landlord, Arthur Veal. We had formed a habit of sitting in front of the fire, his wife sitting peacefully knitting. He had served in the Boar war in Africa and we were mutually interested in each other's experiences. I had found it beneficial to talk about the horrors of the war, letting my feelings out rather than burying them. We were both pipe smokers and much time was spent tamping tobacco in our pipes and generally gazing into the flames, the occasional memory escaping our lips.

'Well now,' he paused taking his pipe from his mouth examining it, as if the answer to the mystery lay there. 'Martha would know more about her.' He turned to his wife who had half an ear to our conversation and had laid down her knitting.

'Nancy? Emma Curnow's girl. My grandmother loved to tell tales of that one, Emma Curnow, Mr Kendrick. She went to school with her. A wild one, she told us. A regular beauty; riding bareback on the moor, hair flying free, meeting young lads up at the stones. Her parents lost control of her, her father even considered putting her away in Bodmin Asylum, but married her off instead, to John Nankervis. He was much older than her but steady, a man of means from Penzance, and he brought her to heel, she told us. It was an ultimatum from her father, that or being sectioned. She was only sixteen, poor child. In those days you could be put away easily, to avoid disgrace to the family, and never seen again.'

'Poor girl. So she was child?' I asked.

'She was. It was taken from her the day it was born, my grandmother said. A girl, and given to the young couple that lived at the time, in that house you have bought.'

It is no exaggeration to say that from that evening, I could not get that young woman out of my mind. Sixteen, with child, married off to a man much older than her who had brought her to heel, in the words of my landlady, her baby girl taken away. She must have known where, for it wasn't a large community. Was she able to see her growing up, watch her playing in the garden from the shelter of the trees. Did she ever think of picking her up and running away? Then, that day that she was buried, just ten years old, did she manage to stand at the back of the mourners, weep and think of what might have been?

I took possession of the house early in September. I had purchased a fine writing desk at an auction in Penzance and placed it in front of the side window that faced onto the churchyard. There was a peace about the view that I found calming, the stones, a robin that perched on one particular one, near the window, eyes darting around and for a moment, I imagined, fixed on me. Blackbirds chased each other furiously among the graves, fighting over territory. I could see the gravestone from there, too and there was something comforting in knowing that I was keeping an eye Emma's baby. Perhaps I hoped that I might see her again but I wouldn't admit that , even to myself.

If I had hoped to sleep soundly, now that I had left everything behind me, I was wrong. I woke frequently often staring into the dark, trying to remember my dream, feeling uneasy, sometimes certain that I had been woken by a sound close by. But only a silence remained, perhaps broken by the sharp cry of a nearby fox seeking a mate, or a tawny owl calling from the wood.

Then one night not long after I moved in, I woke with a start and there standing at the foot of the bed, looking down on me, was a slim figure of a young girl dressed very much as I had seen her that day in the churchyard. The moon was shining through the window lighting up her pale oval face, her hair had fallen loose from under her bonnet and lay over her shoulders. Her eyes were dark, questioning, her hands held out towards me in supplication. I sat up, now fully awake with shock, but there was nothing, only my heart beating loudly in my head.

I lit a candle with shaking hands and for the rest of the night defied sleep, until morning, when I must have eventually succumbed, for I woke late, a rare ray of sun lighting up the window.

I did not disbelieve in ghosts. There had been much talk in the trenches among the lads, of seeing old friends that had vanished in the mud, drowned in the shell holes; ghosts that roamed no-mans land at night trying to find a way home. It was easy, if you had been through what I had, to believe in ghosts; to hope that there was another life going on somewhere; somewhere where human beings were kinder to each other.

During the next few weeks, I made careful enquiries as to whether anyone else had ever experienced such a happening as mine. I had seen her on two occasions now. Cornwall was a place for ghosts; the ghostly engine houses hugging the cliffs, the bare boned remains of wrecked ships, tales of headless highwaymen foretelling death, but try as I might, there was no mention of Emma Curnow haunting the churchyard.

Then I made a discovery that chilled me to the bone. Out of curiosity I had researched early records of deaths around the time that Nancy had died and was ploughing through a copy of 'The Royal Cornwall Gazette,' when a small paragraph under the

heading 'Tragic Suicide,' caught my eye. It was short and to the point,
'It is thought that a young woman of twenty-six years threw herself off the cliff, near Morvah. A lobster fisherman saw her body on the beach below the chapel. It was later confirmed that she was the wife of John Nankervis of Penzance, Emma Nankervis. She had been missing from home for a month and had been seen in the area in the last few days.'

I thought about the words on the gravestone, '*Nancy beloved daughter of Thirza and John Trevarrick.*' How untrue and cruel those few words must have seemed to her; the final straw before she had thrown herself off the cliff onto the rocks below. I knew instantly what I must do. It was as if she had spoken to me. I firmly believed that she had come to me for a purpose. I hired a stonemason, and inventing a connection with Thirza Trevarrick, I persuaded him to add the words, '*Also in remembrance of Emma Curnow, who gave birth to this angel and loved her dearly.*'

Did I imagine it a couple of years later, when I remarried and set off to Australia with my young wife, imagine as I turned with a last look at my old house, a figure in black standing at the gravestone, her head turned towards me, her long black hair lifting with the wind?

A Foggy Day in London Town

I had walked down Bond Street countless times. For one thing it was the way I always took from Harley Street to my club in Piccadilly. Near too, was my tailor in Saville row, and straight ahead, Burlington Arcade, and of course, Hills, halfway down, violin makers. Samuel Pepys had mentioned them in his diary.

I played the viola moderately well in an amateur string quartet in Hampstead. There is nothing so difficult, I think, then merging in with three other different personalities, an elderly friend of my mother on the cello, a young woman violinist, a teacher at the local primary school, who, I must confess, I was desperately in love with, and my mother, on the piano. The very intricacies and challenges that this exercise demanded, helped to transport me from my rather tedious profession as a doctor, in Harley Street

I always paused outside Hills. I loved looking in the old fashioned rounded bow windows to see what instruments they were displaying, often finding an excuse to enter and buy strings, so that I could look at the old instruments in the large glass display cases. Or perhaps brush shoulders with one of the greats. It was, among violinists the world over, the holy of holies.

Naturally, having fallen in love with Rosie, our young violinist, I looked forward eagerly to our weekly meetings, in our rather grand house in Hampstead. Love, such as this, had passed me by up this point in my life. At thirty, I had always seen myself as the confirmed bachelor. The sudden shock of being in love, to me, was rather like throwing a stone into a placid lake and I think the ripples that ensued, jolted me out of the level plain of my existence. I was such a creature of habit, my ordered life indulged by the inherited wealth I had grown up with, my profession, and my love of books and music. Looking back at what happened to me on one particular day in December 1965, may have been the result of one of those ripples as it disturbed the surface of my life.

That day, a very ordinary day, all my appointments finished, I closed my practice and stepped out into Harley Street, looking forward to dinner at my club, a roaring fire and a brandy. To my amazement, a fog lay so thickly over everything, that I could hardly see from one side of the road to the other, and my hope of taking a taxi, was instantly dashed. A fog in November was nothing unusual, but this was so bad that it had brought everything to a halt. The silence was almost deafening. It was another world.

There was only one thing for it, I decided; that was to feel my way through the streets on foot. On a fine day it was an enjoyable walk, up Wimpole Street across Cavendish Square, bearing right down Oxford Street, left down Vere Street, into New Bond street and so on. I had walked it so often that I was confident, that with a little care, I could manage it.

Of course, I could have easily walked north down Harley Street, picked up the underground at Regents Park, changed at Oxford Circus onto the Piccadilly line to Green Park, although I could not know, that, because the fog had seeped down into the tunnels that criss-crossed London like spiderwebs, the trains had also been brought to a halt.

Wimpole Street was fairly straightforward, although it seemed a little unfamiliar, but then the fog tends to turn everything into unfamiliar territory. Crossing Cavendish Square was a little difficult. I groped my way to the Jockey Club, steps, then headed straight across the road, tripping over the payment, very nearly knocking down a young lady, who seized my arm, appealing for help.

'I am completely lost, I'm afraid,' she laughed.

After apologising profusely, I asked her where she was going.

'Wigmore Hall,' she replied.

'Oh, that's easy. Straight along there,' I pointed into the fog, where I thought Wigmore Street must be, then hesitated.

'Look, I'll take you. It's only a little way and I know this area well,' I offered. 'Take my arm.'

'You are kind,' she said softly, slipping her arm through mine.

Slowly we made our way along Wigmore Street, hugging the railings. Soon the Hall, loomed up out of the fog; I opened the door for her and followed her into the foyer.

'Thank you so much,' she said. 'I hope that it's not cancelled,' she added, removing her wide brimmed hat. Thick long black hair parted either side of her face, falling over her shoulders.

'What's the programme?' I asked, just to delay my departure, for I could see now that she was exceedingly beautiful, narrow waist, a long black coat, reaching her ankles, just the very tips of her shoes showing

'Beethoven and Schumann,' she said, removing her gloves. 'I'm a pianist. I have been so looking forward to this.'

'Have you come far?' I asked. 'It's a real pea-souper. Quite unusual, these days.'

She smiled. 'Luckily I was staying at Claridges overnight. It would have been impossible from home, Hampstead. It appears the underground has been closed.'

She really was very beautiful. Eighteen or so. I thought.

On an impulse, I felt in my pocket and handed her my card.

'Oh, look. I live in Hampstead, too. I play in a quartet, Viola, and we are looking for a pianist. My mother, who is very talented, is finding it difficult these days. You know arthritis. It creeps up on you.' I smiled. 'But then you wouldn't know about that. If you are ever, you know, at a loose end,' I ended lamely, feeling a bit of a fool.

She laughed. 'I will remember that. Thank you. I have a spare programme,' she added, handing it to me. 'Why don't you stay? I believe there are seats available.'

I was sorely tempted but I had to buy late Christmas presents for my mother and Rosie, our violinist. I knew which scent Rosie liked and intended to drop in at Selfridges on my way to my club.

'I'd love to but, you know, late Christmas shopping, and all that.'

She laughed. 'My father's the same. My mother's organised. Starts in October. Well, look I must go. Thank you once again. You have been most kind.'

I glanced at my watch, as I reluctantly wished her goodbye. She was certainly early for the performance, at least a couple of hours, I thought, as I emerged into Oxford Street and turned for Selfridges.

The fog was just as thick, here, buses had stopped for there was none in sight. I found that I had wandered off the pavement, for a horse and carriage, to my horror, suddenly loomed out of the fog, the two black horses blowing hard, eyes glaring, the driver shouting at me to get out of the way. I groped my way back to the pavement, shaken up a little, and came face to face with scaffolding and building works.

As far as I could see, there was an enormous building being constructed, where Selfridges normally stood, unless I was somewhere else entirely. I stopped and tried calming myself. I was lost. How could I be?' I asked myself, crossing the road, fearing that any minute I might be run down, but silence had descended again, but for the fading hooves of the carriage horses. A feeling of unreality seeped over me; a carriage with two great horses!

A dim light beckoned and I was thankful to make out a small public house, not one I was familiar with, but then London was always throwing up surprises. It was devoid of people. I ordered a meal, from a young man at the bar, knowing that it was useless to proceed further, hoping the fog would lift, before long.

It was some time later. I must have fallen asleep in the snug, in front of the fire. I glanced at the clock on the wall. It was half past nine.

'You were well away,' the landlady smiled, when I went to the bar to pay for my meal. 'We thought we'd leave you.'

I glanced around me at the sound of voices. Noise and laughter, quite a crowd. I felt in my pocket for my wallet, still half asleep and the programme, that the young lady had given me, dropped out onto the floor I bent to pick it up. A picture of a young woman on the front. I rubbed my eyes. It was her. The young woman I had met in Cavendish Square

Slowly I read, '*Beethoven and Schumann Piano Sonatas. Debut recital by Myra Hess, 21st December 1907'*.

You alright sir?' the landlady asked.

'Myra Hess!' I exclaimed, stupidly.

The landlady had her back to me, calculating my bill.

'Such a loss,' she said. 'We were so upset when she died last month. Of course you are too young, but we heard her play several times. She did so much in the war, you know, to keep our spirits up. I don't think there will be another like her. Now, let's see. A lightly done steak and chips, wasn't it?'

'Has the fog cleared?' I asked, still in shock, folding the programme carefully, replacing it my pocket.

'Fog sir? Why it's been fine all day. Chilly, but I always think it's nice to see the sun this time of the year, don't you? Makes you think Spring isn't too far away.'

Postscript:
Dame Julia Myra Hess, DBE was a world famous English pianist, best known for her performances of the works of Bach, Mozart, Beethoven and Schumann
Born: February 25, 1890, Hampstead. Died: November 25, 1965
Selfridges Oxford Street opened 16th March 1909

The Rose of Carlisle.

I boarded the 'Rose of Carlisle,' in Shanghai on the 26th May 1860, bound for London. Our cargo of tea already aboard, we were soon towed out into clear water of the Yangtze river. The crew set all the sails, a brisk breeze filling the enormous canvases, and we began to move, gathering speed as we made for open water of the China Sea. 14000 miles and 100 days, or so, lay ahead and always, always, Cape Horn and the roaring forties.

The 'Rose of Carlisle' was built for speed, expressly to get the tea shipment to London in the shortest possible time. It was a race that spared no -one. Below decks were stacked 12,000 tea chests and above decks 26,000 square feet of canvas, that drew us onwards, towards the Horn, at 16 knots.

This would probably be my last voyage on a tea clipper. My father had died back in England and I needed to take over the estate in Kent and take care of my mother. It would be a huge change from managing the plantation, but for a long time now, I had been longing for home and the milder climate.

The first mate showed me to my cabin, informing me that they were an officer short, so luckily a cabin spare. It was nothing more than a small cupboard, really. I was not looking forward to the next hundred days or so. The captain, of the 'Rose', John Knight, had informed me that I was the only passenger on board. I had the impression, that even then, I was one too many. An idle man on a ship that has been paired down in weight to gain speed, wasn't welcome. But then he had no choice. I held shares in the 'Rose.' She was a beauty, narrow beam, a four master, built in the same yard in Denbighshire as the Cutty Sark, which was to emerge into the tea trade, later.

I had decided to sell my shares when I reached London. The Suez Canal had just opened up, the future almost certainly in steam ships. The estate would need money. My mother had informed me that little had been spent these last few years. There was always the land. My father had been reluctant to sell land. I might have to.

I felt the beginning of a swell beneath my feet, while the wind in the rigging had increased. I packed my things away and climbed up onto the poop deck. The sky was darkening and the tips of the waves were showing white; a force six, I reckoned, thinking that if it only stopped at that over the next three months, we would be lucky, but at the Horn the wind was rarely below a force ten and mostly above eleven or even twelve, over a hundred miles an hour.

I had sailed around the Horn only once, when I had left England for Shanghai. We had battled for hours against the westerlies and rounded the huge rock, at last in a force nine gale, that was deemed to be moderate by the crew.

We docked in the Port of London, ninety-six days later, four days earlier than our rival clipper.

How can I tell you the hardships and horrors of those ninety-six days? Rounding the Horn in a force eleven gale, when for a long period, the upper decks were under water and we thought that our end had come. Somehow, we came through it. Afterwards we sailed through much calmer water, spurred on by the roaring forties up the coast of Africa, repairing the damage as best we could. I willingly helped, glad to have obtained the respect of the crew, for going aloft at the height of the gale and helping to reduce sail.

The day that we docked, I accompanied John Knight to a nearby Inn, for a meal, where I hoped to stay the night. We had become friends during the voyage, enjoying a game of chess in calmer seas. In the quiet of the snug, enjoying the luxury of a well-cooked steak, he asked me, to my surprise, if I had seen her. For a moment I was taken aback, then I met his eyes and nodded.

'I thought so,' he smiled. 'She was a daughter of Captain Henry Marsh, who was my predecessor; the first master of the 'Rose.' The ship was named after her, Rose Marsh. He brought his family on board, before she made her maiden voyage. Rose, very high spirited, climbed a little way up the rigging, when they were not looking and fell twenty foot onto the deck. Just twelve years old and their only child. It broke them. Henry insisted on sailing. He was a hard man. He never came back. Couldn't face it and it was said that he committed suicide. Rose has been seen several times but only by certain people. I have never seen her and can only take the word of others but believe me, I have seen such things over the years to know that nothing is impossible.'

I described the young girl that I had seen, when we were nearing Cape Horn. The crew, all twenty-four of them, were changing the summer sails for heavier stronger canvas, swarming in the top yards, singing and laughing, probably, underneath, trying to push the approaching Cape Horn to the back of their minds.

I stood looking up, watching them, the sun on my face, when suddenly, I knew that I was not alone. I turned. A young girl stood not four yards away her eyes on the topsails, her hands folded in front of her, a smile on her lips; pretty, curly blonde hair escaping from under her bonnet. As I stared at her, dumbfounded, she met my eyes smiling, such a sweet smile, so like my sister, who, at much the same age, had died of diphtheria that I stepped towards her. At this moment a heavy marlin spike hit the deck behind me. I stared down at it in horror, realising that I could have been killed, if I had not moved. When I looked up she was no more.

The remainder of the day, I was in a daze. I thought about going to Captain Knight, but something in me spoke of caution. I felt that I would be ridiculed and accused of spreading alarm. Already some of the crew regarded me with suspicion and I wasn't at all sure that the near brush with death, that I had experienced, was an accident. Isolated with twenty or so other men for three months, was hardly the situation in which to stir up feelings. I knew how easy sailors came to regard anyone different to them as Jonahs; bringers of bad luck.

Then I saw her again, during the height of the storm when we were within a hundred yards, or so, of the great rock, the Horn. By then two men had been washed overboard, despite every effort to save them, and the main mast was coming under pressure. Our only hope was to reduce sail. I was up on the royal yards, the very highest point in the ship, the deck below looking like a distant handkerchief, trying to bring in the gallant sails, with ten others, the heavy canvas billowing and threatening to whip us off into the raging sea.

I had climbed up the rigging with them, never for one moment thinking of the height and the fierce wind threatening to pluck us off, back onto the deck far below. When you think you are going to die anyway, then nothing else seems to matter. As I threw myself over a yard arm, grappling with the canvas, I looked down and there she was on the anchor deck far below, watching us. The wind dropped suddenly for a moment and we were able to secure the largest of the royals. I looked again, and after a moment she turned away. A huge wave came over the gunwale and she was hidden from sight. When the water cleared, there was nothing, just the empty deck. For the rest of the voyage, I constantly looked for her to no avail.

John Knight listened to me patiently as the evening drew in, nodding at my description of the girl. The landlord came in remarking on the chill of the evening and put a match to the pile of logs, the flames eventually flickering on the walls, the rain beating on the windows. I could still feel the floor moving under my feet.

'Your sister?' John asked quietly, after a while. 'Was she of a similar age?'

'Yes. She reminded me of her,' I answered, lifting the mug of ale to my lips. 'I still miss her after all this time.'

'Mm. It is thought by those that have seen Rose, that she appears only to those, who have had great sadness in their lives; that she is of a protective nature.'

He laughed. 'There are so many such tales of the sea.' He sighed. 'Well I gather you are staying the night here before continuing your journey home? There is someone waiting for you, I trust.'

'My mother and younger brother and a cousin, I grew up with.'

I smiled. 'We vowed when we were little that one day we would marry each other. Perhaps the time has come.'

He rose and took my hand. 'I hope so. It's been a pleasure knowing you.'

I never saw him again. Some years later, I read in 'The Times' that 'The Rose of Carlisle' had foundered off the Horn, all hands lost.

That night, lying sleepless, my wife by my side, I thought of John Knight and the crew of the Rose, and of Rose Marsh. It was Sunday. After the service in the little church on the estate, I would light a candle for them all and another one for Rose Marsh and my sister. Then we would, as a family, walk on the downs, above our house, where we could get a glimpse of the sea.

The Blue Dress.

I am not at all certain that I should be setting this down on paper but it has been on my mind for a very long time and I hope that by telling the tale, I will in some sense, at least, disperse the feeling of dread I still experience when I enter that part of the world. Of course, it would be better, some would argue, if I avoided the place at all cost, but I am strangely drawn there, sometimes through unavoidable circumstances connected with my profession.

I work as a technical officer for Ordnance Survey. I won't go into the various projects I have to undertake but a great deal of it is checking on previously amassed data sometimes in libraries and more often out in the field. I love walking and the open air and often congratulate myself on my luck in pursuing a profession that sometimes seems to be more of a holiday rather than a job. Of course, there are days when routine sets in and I long to be out there away from the stuffy office but all in all they are quite few.

My region, the area I am responsible for, is what is known as the Welsh Marches which in medieval times divided England from Wales, a collection of giant gaunt castles and mysterious dark villages that were neither Welsh or English and where in the dark ages, their inhabitants lived a strange in-between life of intrigue and deception and ultimate survival. I was, on the whole, very content with the area that I had under my control; it was well documented and the history was fascinating but of course my job did not concern the history of the area as such but only the records that had been amassed over the years concerning what my boss referred to as the 'attributes'; the footpaths, ancient rights of way, the green roads and the old tracks, long vanished in the bracken and newly grown copses of silver birch that obliterated anything that spoke of a another age, a different way of life. I carried with me a digitised collection of early maps from the 1840s and more often than not my predecessors had done a fine job in recording strange diversions and antiquities but every so often I made a discovery and that was the excitement of the job; it wasn't as if that revelation would ever bear my name as a botanist might experience in discovering a new species but nevertheless it was an achievement.

It was a lonely job and often I would spend a day without seeing another soul; sometimes I slept in inns rather than to return to my local office in Shrewsbury. It was very much a part of England that still held distinct echoes of the distant past and often after a day alone one could be excused for imagining that one had slipped into another age.

One of my interests were ram pumps; I had an ear for them and they were much more prolific than one imagined. In fact, they were of very little consequence in the general run of things but they were worth recording and were usually to be found by necessity quite close to an old dwelling that in itself had long disappeared even as far back to the early 1800s. These simple metal machines often worked on regardless of any need still fed by an upland stream thudding rhythmically on with a deep throbbing sound. I won't go into the simple mechanics of the machine and how it supplies water upwards for some miles for that would be straying away from the direction of this narrative. They were invented in 1790 and James Easton of Easton and Amos purchased the patent in the early 1800s and distributed them all over England; later they were improved by Green and Carter but it was possible to still find these very early examples, possible but in truth very rarely did they come to the surface; they were buried deep beneath years of fallen leaves and shifting soil and their thudding hearts had long ceased to function. You could find them in museums but they were extremely rare and my dream was to one day come across one in my wanderings.

I mention this interest in ram pumps simply because it was what ultimately led me to the burial ground.

It was a dark day with heavy black clouds scudding low overhead and the occasional short sharp icy shower. I had stayed in a 16th century inn some twenty miles south of Ludlow; it was an area that I had neglected, difficult to reach by train and bus, my usual form of transports. I left the car at home as it, to my mind inhibited exploration, being too easy to pass things by and return to.

At the Inn over a hearty breakfast in front of a roaring log fire I argued that it would be sensible on such a day to return to Shrewsbury by the earliest train and work on the material I had already gathered, such as it was. I do though have a stubborn streak, or so my wife tells me and I felt a need to complete my survey. I was due a holiday and I was aware that I had been overworking; trying to complete an area that had so far eluded me; parcel it up in a box and store it away; this on reflection may have been the reason for my experience that day; over tiredness. But who knows? I have a feeling that it was out there waiting for me and had always been so.

Once a long time ago when I was in my early twenties I came across a large ornamental headstone in a cemetery in London; a young girl of thirteen years who had died in 1755; her name was Harriet Verity. It had been dreadfully neglected. The inscription read - ‘She who loved this earth so much is now at peace with it and in her makers hands.’ I was so moved by this that for some time during my stay in London I visited the grave and placed flowers upon it. In fact, I became a little obsessed as is my wont and dug out all the information I could find on Harriet Verity. It seemed that she was the only daughter of a very rich family who had resided in Ludlow and had moved to London in 1750. Particularly beautiful and talented her life had been cut off cruelly by diphtheria. There was a large Manor house near Ludlow that was marked on the OS map and had, in the 1600s to 1700s, been the residence of the Verity family. It was now in National Trusts hands and an oil painting of Harriet when she was ten years old by Richard Wilson was on show with her parents. On that day I stood for some time in front of it noting the light in her eyes and the expectation of life ahead which she must have been feeling; it made the occasion all the sadder but in a strange way a culmination of all that had gone before. Little did I think on that dark day, all those years later when I set out from the 'The Black Lion that I would meet Harriet Verity not exactly in the flesh but of some diaphanous substance.

It was some four hours later. I had followed an old green way that led into thickly wooded hills when I heard the ram pump; just an occasional thud. I studied my map and saw that there was no record of one or of a dwelling nearby ancient or otherwise. Excitement mounting, I made my way through thick undergrowth and then glimpsed the top of the ram glistening with a recent shower just emerging through the autumn leaves; part of the river bank had slipped away with the recent rain and had left it partly exposed. I fumbled in my rucksack and slipped a pair of gardening gloves on, that I always carried with me. I dug around the spherical dome; every now and then it vibrated as the water built up inside it and caused the valve to open releasing its load upwards to some mysterious destination. To my amazement and utter joy, the legend 'James Easton and Amos' appeared in bold letters. I stared at it for some minutes my heart beating uncomfortably determined that I would return another day and somehow excruciate it from the earth and take it home. Then it occurred to me that it had at one time been the only supply of fresh water to some cottage or other and that first I must find out if the cottage still existed. I uncovered the supply pipe and noting in which direction it was travelling made my way slowly and with great difficulty through the undergrowth, briars clinging to my legs and pulling at my clothes as if to deter me, at all cost, to continue my quest. As I progressed uphill stumbling over hidden roots I was suddenly aware that an uncanny silence had fallen around me and a sense of uneasiness came over me. I was after all miles from anywhere and it was unlikely that there was any habitation nearby, despite the presence of the ram pump. This sense of uneasiness increased as I struggled on and I was in half a mind to turn back. They say that in humans there is an innate sense of evil an innate sense of disaster looming that protects us. Some of the soldiers in the First World War experienced such an emotion and put it down to saving their lives.

This sense of evil, I can say now, was nothing that I had ever experienced before and hope to never again. How can I describe it? Like a black creeping icy mist rising ever higher around one's body taking ones breath chilling ones very bones. I stopped and listened; still not a sound now; the wind that had been quite blustery all morning had dropped.; the only movement were of leaves dropping off the trees. Another few steps and I was in a small clearing and in front of me a ruined church and a graveyard.

It was then that I saw her standing by a tombstone. I called out her name as if I had known her all my life and she turned towards me, her pale face full of foreboding. She was dressed like her portrait in a long satin blue dress; her hair golden, tumbling over her shoulders; she shook her head and crossed her arms in front of her breast as if in warning and gradually faded away, leaving me shocked and breathless; suddenly there were sounds all around me as if soldiers were moving through the trees, the occasional clank of swords and armour. I turned and ran in terror as well as I was able back through the way I had come sustaining much bruising and scratches to my face and arms before I was once more back in the lane. A blackbird alarmed nearby and a robin sang and soon calmness and the sense of well-being was restored.

There was no record of what had happened there many years ago; perhaps no-one had remained alive to tell the tale. The church and the ram pump did not exist on any map and I decided to leave it that way. I visit the ram pump occasionally. It is best left where it is. It is now ten years since I discovered it and I am due for retirement. Occasionally there is the intermittent thud as I stand over it, admiring it's sleekness and antiquity, but they are becoming less and soon I know it's heart will stop forever. The last time I went I covered it over so that it would never be discovered and torn from the ground; it will remain my secret and of course Harriet's. Something we can share.

I never saw Harriet again. Once standing by the ram pump I imagined I caught a flash of a blue dress through the trees but I couldn't be sure. I like to think that she is looking out for me in my old age.

The Clock.

The grandfather clock had been quite reasonable, considering it's age and condition, I thought. I had spotted it in the auction catalogue, sent to me monthly from Sotherbys of London. It was a particularly good specimen, a 19th century English Longcase, about 1820, with a wonderful painted dial with a working moon feature signed by a Sam Collier of Eccles.

It was something I had been hoping to find for some time and knew immediately that it would fit well into my house in Tonbridge in Kent, a rambling affair on the outskirts of the town, with its 18th century baroque. I loved it's dark Gothic atmosphere, the manner with which it responded to the wind and the rain, a living thing that had grown over the centuries, and because of the ample means I had at my disposal, since my retirement as a magistrate, I had filled it with the baroque antiques that I loved.

As a bachelor of some years, I had no need to answer to anyone, other than my housekeeper, Mrs Francis, so without more ado I caught the early milk train for London and after breakfast in Claridges, I was able to examine the clock, aided by a particularly attractive young lady assistant, of which there are many in such institutions, expressly to charm an old man like me.

A fine mahogany case, with satinwood inlay, a beautiful painted dial with subsidiary dials and a working moon with painted face, a sailing ship, and blue sea. An eight-day movement with low rich chime denoting every hour. I was entranced. I left a bid far in excess of the reserve price and what the assistant thought it might fetch, so it was in the hands of the gods, whether or not I would become the owner of the clock. I was not inclined to be present at the auction as I found them, to be noisy and exhausting these days and no longer enjoyed the excitement, as I had done in the past.

A week later I received a letter from Sotherbys to say that, indeed, the clock was mine and that they would be obliged if I would settle with them, upon which they would deliver it to me by carrier. I had been a valued customer of theirs, over the years, and the cost for carriage was extremely reasonable.

My house was panelled with dark oak throughout, a curved oak staircase, a mahogany hand rail and a large newel post topped by a finial that was either carved by Grinling Gibbons or was certainly of the Grinling Gibbons school; this was the first of many such treasures that met ones eye, as one entered the heavy baroque front door, into the hall. An intricate merging of interweaving branches and leaves, a child's face, peering through the vegetation as if caught hiding. I had studied his work in my lunch hours, while a young man, training to be a barrister in the City churches. For insurance purposes an expert from the V&A had examined it minutely but could not come to any conclusion. Nevertheless, Grinling Gibbons, or not, it was very much admired by my friends.

It was here in the hall, at the bottom of the staircase, that I decided to place my newly acquired longcase clock.

I was fond of walking and spent a great deal of my time outdoors, which accounted for my fitness, often remarked upon by those that did not lead such healthy lives. Upon entering my front door, I would see the clock and in time honoured manner, draw out my fob watch and check the time. I loved that sort of ritual. It seemed to state to me that everything in the world was as it should be.

And so it became a part of the house and a part of my life. Where it had been since leaving the workshops of Sam Collier of Eccles in 1820, I had no idea, for it owned no provenance, unusual as that may seem, for normally such creations are well documented.

At first, I loved the slow sound of the clock ticking away the hours and it's deep sonorous chime, which faintly reached me in the drawing room where I sat at my writing desk; no other sounds reached me, and I had always loved the silence of the house except for the creaking's and groanings in inclement weather, which to me was part of its nature, almost part of the silence itself.

The beat of Sam Collier's clock was hardly noticeable during the first few weeks and seemed to enhance the rhythm with which my writing progressed. I wrote a nature column for the Times, which involved my daily wanderings and the things I saw changing in the fields and hedgerows as the seasons unfolded. I liked to think I was a latent Richard Jeffries but knew that I had not the skill of observation, that he had possessed

Naturally, my housekeeper, Mrs Francis did not enhance the silence of the house as she busied herself, keeping everything clean neat and tidy, so it was that, when she returned to the village, her husband and children, mid-afternoon, having prepared my evening meal to heat up later, I sighed with relief, and let the silence once more fold itself around me, reading or dozing in front of the fire, listening to the odd sounds of the house talking to me, or that's how I liked to think of them.

It was some months after purchasing my clock, that I noticed a change. The movement was louder and the chime more resonant. I remarked on it to Mrs Francis but she thought it was much the same as it had been. It was at night that I noticed it more as the days wore on and found that I was lying awake, waiting for the hourly chime.

Soon it became so intolerable that I was unable to write. The only escape I had was leaving the house and the clock behind but even then, it seemed to stay with me. I had noticed that the beat of the clock was in exact time with the beat of my heart, which at times was disconcerting. A solution had to be found and much against my better nature, one evening, I opened the little front door, reached inside the clock's innards and removed the pendulum. I poured a brandy, my hand shaking, and stood contemplating the clock, silent, its hands at half past seven, hands which would remain at half past seven, until the day I died as I had no intention of restoring its life, for such a mechanism is a living thing, whatever it is, a watch, a mantle clock or anything that has such an intricate system of tiny wheels, springs, guvnors or pendulums, and to bring them to a halt was rather like taking their life away. Murder. It was still very much a thing of beauty and I consoled myself with that thought, as I made my way to bed that night. I no sooner put my head on the pillow and drifted off into a slightly troubled sleep when I woke with a start. The moon was throwing a silver river across the floor, and up the wall onto my bookcase and a bronze of Diana, the huntress, two large dogs at her hands straining on a leash. I sat up, aware that something had happened. Then I heard it. One chime, then a steady loud beat getting louder by the second, as if it was climbing the stairs tread by tread. Then the door flew open. A cloud suddenly extinguished the moon and I was left in darkness. I will not relate the terror I felt in the next few minutes; the beat reached a crescendo and then gradually abated until all was quiet again

My doctor said it was my heart, when he took my blood pressure the next day.

'Quite a common complaint at your age,' he said, replacing his stethoscope, in his bag 'Pulsatile Tinnitus. I'll give you something to lower your blood pressure. May help.'

When he had gone, I removed the pendulum for the second time, packing it securely in tissue and cardboard, placing it back inside the clock and arranged for Sotherbys to collect it.

The house was never the same. I sold it six months later and with the proceeds, went abroad on my doctor's advice, taking an apartment in Venice, where I bathed on the balcony in the morning sun and toured the galleries in the afternoon. Much is to be said for it.

The Mountain Road.

I arrived late at the small welsh village of Llanbedow. The narrow street was deserted, as I drove towards the square, a few windows lit up; a glimpse of a Christmas tree, coloured lights flickering.

The lights of the village inn shone brightly and the sound of laughter, for a moment, was a temptation, but I knew that with twelve miles of mountain road ahead, a trailer with two ponies, behind my land rover, I had to push on. Besides the snow had definitely begun to settle and I was longing to get home, bed the ponies down and sit down to a hot meal, before a roaring fire with my wife and daughters. They would be waiting patiently now, excited at the thought of seeing their ponies again, listening for every sound that might announce my arrival. Looking forward to Christmas morning, our first Christmas in Wales.

I should have been there now, but for a holdup over a fallen tree. A gale had been raging all afternoon, making life very difficult. I thought about phoning my wife as I passed the call box in the square but I knew that she would persuade me to leave the journey until the next day, but I wanted to be home for Christmas morning.

We had moved from Reading late in November, leaving the ponies with a friend. It had been an easy decision to make. I had been offered a warden's post on a bird reserve, with a lovely cottage thrown in. It was something I had been waiting for all my life and had come at a time when my youngest daughter was recovering from cancer. Thankfully she had won through and we still had her, although the worry was still there and with the sale of our house, we had the money for further treatment, if necessary. We could not contemplate the sheer trauma of losing her and hung desperately on to the belief that this fresh start in our lives, would be the solution.

I knew the mountain road quite well. We had spent our holidays with my wife's sister and her husband, who lived in nearby Builth Wells, where my wife had been born. They had two girls as well and our children had all grown up together. The first two miles of the mountain road was the worst bit, rising very steeply, almost one in four, needing a quick change into first gear with this load behind me. Once over that I would be alright, so without more ado, and a last look at the tempting lights of the inn, I turned onto the mountain road.

Soon, all too soon, I reached the steepest part of the road, that I had been dreading, and slipped into first gear a little late, so that the rover almost came to a halt, wheels slipping on the ice and snow, but then began to climb slowly on up. I hardly dare to think of the trailer dragging us backwards. We reached the top of the hill, the slope evened out and I breathed easier. A barn owl flew out of the trees on my right and across my path, sometime later. Immediately in my mind I was seeking a possible roost. There was a path through the forestry, that we had walked, in past summers; a large barn and a farm on the open upland. I would bring the girls up here tomorrow. We could all come after Christmas dinner. We may be lucky enough to see the owl skimming low over the fields, I thought. Red Kites up above lazily circling; the odd Buzzard. Suddenly I felt happier, the worry of the last few months lifting slightly.

It was at this moment that disaster struck. Out of the protection of the trees, a sudden strong gust of wind hit us, the trailer skewing sideways coming very close to the edge of the road with a thirty foot drop on to the river below. I tried to drive on but the wheels slipped on the ice beneath the thin covering of snow. I got out and studied the situation, the wind roaring in my ears, the snow beginning to thicken.

'You'll have to get the ponies out,' A voice shouted in my ear and I felt a light touch on my shoulder. My heart thumping I looked around. A young man, holding on to the hand of a child, stood smiling at me. ‘ Don’t worry. I’ll help. We’ll have you back on the road in no time.’

I looked down at the child. It was a girl, about the same age as my youngest, nine or ten. The girl let go of his hand and came to me. I took the hand that was offered. It was ice cold.

‘You shouldn’t be out in this,’ I shouted at him, above the wind, as he let down the ramp of the trailer.

‘Nor should you,’ he replied, leading one of the ponies out and handing the halter to me. The girl looked up at me and I held her gaze for a moment, smiling down at her, she made no response. Such a serious little face.

‘Hullo, I said. She must be frozen, I thought. How could he be so stupid to bring her out in this? I thought of my own daughters at home waiting for me, warm in front of the fire.

‘There! I heard him say, handing the other halter to me.

I heard him put the ramp up. ‘It should pull free now easily. Just hold on to those and I’ll get it straight.’

‘Let me do it,’ I said.

‘No I’m used to this road, it could still go over the edge if we are not careful.’

Suddenly I realised that the girl was no longer at my side. I had let go of her hand as I took the ponies. I looked around, for her but the ponies pulled at me and it was all I could do to hang onto them. Normally calm and well behaved, their ears were laid back, eyes wide with fear.

He eased the rover forward and the trailer out of danger, then he was back by my side.

‘You drive on a bit,’ he said. I’ll walk them. Once you are past this bit it’s easy going and safe.’

‘Your daughter!’ I gasped. ‘She’s gone.’

‘I have no daughter,’ he said quietly.

‘But, but she was here. I held her hand.’ I protested.

He looked away. ‘Must be your imagination. This road does funny things to people.’

He took the ponies from me, meeting my eyes. 'I have no daughter,' he said again. 'Drive on for half a mile to the cattle grid. I'll catch you up. We'll be out of the wind there. It's safer this way.'

'But -.'

He smiled. 'Go on with you. I'll follow.'

The moment the ponies were in his hands they grew quieter as he calmed them with soft words in welsh.

In a daze, not knowing what to think, I drove on to the cattle grid and waited, keeping the engine running. I had not imagined the girl. How could I, her hand in mine? A shiver ran down my spine. Such a serious little face and such icy hands. Eventually I saw him coming, in the wing mirror and let down the ramp. We loaded the ponies up, fastening the ramp.

'Well, I'll leave you, he said. 'You'll be fine now.'

'I can't thank you enough,' I said, holding out my hand. Come into the cab for a moment. I've a thermos there. It's still hot.'

We sat silently for a while each with his own thoughts warming our hands on the mugs.

'Where do you live?'

'Just a little way back.'

'That farm off the road with the big barn?'

'That's it. Pont Neweth.'

'Look, came back with me. Get a hot meal down you. You must be frozen.'

'No I must get back. My wife will be worried.'

'Call in sometime then. The warden's cottage.'

'I will, thank you,' he said.

'It's five years to the day, that I lost her,' he said, meeting my eyes.

'Who?' I asked, but I knew, only too well.

'My daughter, Bethan. Three years old. She disappeared in weather like this, Christmas Eve. I still look for her. My wife won't talk about her. Feels guilty leaving the door open. Crazy isn't it?'

'No, I said. 'You have to go on searching else nothing else matters.'

'That's what I think. Look, I have never told this to anyone, so why I am telling you, practically a stranger, I don't know. Sometimes, I imagine I can feel her hand in mine. That's why I go on. I don't want that to stop.' He paused and we were silent for a moment. 'It's helped talking to you. Thank you. Look I must get on. Drop in if you ever up there. There's an owl in the barn. They nest there. Keeps the rats down. See you around.'

Then, he was gone into the swirling snow. I could see his figure in the wing mirror, head down, trudging away. I prayed that she would take his hand before he reached home. I was sure she would.

I waited awhile, calming myself, then drove across the cattle grid. Soon I could see the lights of my house twinkling through the beating snow. I had a very strong feeling that everything was going to be alright. I was certain of it.

The Roman Well.

I had been here for just a week. A rambling great house on the Sussex Downs; a retirement home.

It was costing me a lot of money, it was dark, like descending into a previous age, the passages narrow and sometimes seemingly leading nowhere, the furniture heavy. Outside the sea lay at the bottom of an extensive lawn with a sheer drop to the beach below. Obviously fearing that most of the inhabitants would willingly throw themselves into the void, given the chance, a very secure fence had been built to avoid that possibility.

During the Great War of 1914 -18, it had been used as a hospital and my own father had spent some months here after being wounded on the Western Front. As a young boy, he had told me horrific tales of the injuries that the young men had suffered. It was as if he felt that I had to know, despite my mother's qualms regarding my tender young age. He firmly believed that the more everyone knew of the horrors of war the less likely it would happen again. Actually I liked to hear his tales of the war and knew that it helped him to talk about it. There is no doubt that bottling everything up inside, is the worst possible scenario.

'You have to let it all out,' he used to say, when my mother rebuked him.

Sometimes he used to go quiet, when talking about Wallbrooke Hall, meeting my eyes, his face a little pale.

'There are things, son, that I can never tell you.' He would whisper eventually, glancing around, as if someone might hear him. 'They're best forgotten.'

But he could not forget them, and I used to hear him groaning in the night, my mother soothing him back to sleep.

Now in my seventies, my parents long gone, my own strength fading, I had ended up in the very same place, that my father had spent recovering during the Great War. It was no coincidence. He had seen something here, during those seven months, not only the suffering of others but something that he could not tell me about; something that was far from reality. I believe it was why he found comfort, in talking about reality, however horrific it had been.

Wallbrooke Hall, I had discovered, had a strange history. It was built by an Adam Taylor in 1662, the country still recovering from the ravages of the Civil War. Adam Taylor was a philanthropist, a humanitarian, a father of two girls. Adam and his wife Emma, gave sanctuary to those that had nothing and nowhere to lay their head, building cottages in the extensive grounds of their estate, giving work and shelter to those that had fallen upon misfortune.

As the years went by, his two daughters trod the same path that their father and mother had chosen. Adam died in his eighties his wife soon after, and the two girls, mature women now, ran a sanctuary for fallen women, in the Hall, living, themselves, in what used to be the servants quarters.

The house survived the great storm of 1703, a cyclone, which swept England, inflicting enormous damage, but two huge oaks near the house were toppled, revealing a three hundred foot deep well that the Romans had sunk into the chalk a thousand years or so, ago. There were no springs in the locality and water had always been brought from a large dew pond, so the well had been a welcome discovery, except that it became the scene of a violent and horrific occasion, ten years later in 1713.

It was common in those time that the occasional French boat would stand offshore and its crew make raids on property along the south coast, despite the patrols of militia.

It was thought, that such a raid in 1713, on Wallbrooke Hall, took place, a group of Frenchmen, raping two young girls, sisters, tying their hands, before throwing them down the well.

The other women escaped, hiding in cupboards and barns and the extensive attics that ran throughout the building.

When I read this account, in the history of Wallbrooke Hall, an icy shiver ran down my spine. Perhaps this was what my father had not wanted to talk about. It was said in the account that the ghosts of the two girls had been seen on several occasions over the years. Had he seen them? Had he woken in the night to find them standing at his bedside, one each side, their eyes beseeching him for help. If he had, I knew that they would come to me too, for was I not kin? They say that ghosts are attracted to a particular person. Was I that person? From then on, my nights were uneasy ones.

I sought further information in the archives at Arundel. The incident was well documented and a later account gave a more accurate rendering. Two young sisters, Anne and Hannah Kemp, scullery maids, had been raped and dragged from the house in the middle of the afternoon, their hands tied and then thrown down the well. It was witnessed by an Eliza Jenner who had hidden in the huge copper boiler in the wash house. James Baldwin, a magistrate at the time, who had written up the document, suggested that the almost ritualistic nature of the horrendous crime was planned and not a random one. It appeared that the sisters had a brother serving in the British army who had recently been executed for raping and murdering a French girl in the village of Petain, on the French coast. It was not uncommon at this time, with the French and British at each other's throats, that tit for tat crimes of this kind were perpetuated. Nothing was stolen and no other women were harmed, which seemed to justify Baldwins theory

An attempt to recover the bodies of the sisters was made, but the well was far too deep and eventually sealed up with a granite slab depicting the names of the two girls, their dates of birth and the manner in which they were so cruelly murdered. They were barely sixteen and fifteen. Flowers were placed annually on the stone, until the cliff, over the years, ate it's way inland and the stone and the well fell into the sea, the shaft visible as a cleft in the cliff for some years afterwards. A search was made for the remains of the girls, soon after the cliff fall, so that they might receive a Christian burial, but none were found.

Needless to say, this newly acquired knowledge began to occupy my mind, above my own uncomfortable situation; loss of independence, and failing health. These things, which had been uppermost in my mind, dwindled into insignificance, when I thought of those poor innocent children paying the price for their brother's sins. I wished for some form of reparation for them.

Perhaps it was the passion which I felt, that brought about a conclusion. A conclusion that took me to the extreme limits of fear and a belief that good in the end would always prevail.

One evening, I was taking my usual stroll in the grounds, before settling for the night with my book, supper and bed. The sun had just set and it was a time of half-light, the time between light and dark, when anything can happen, or so it is said. The swallows that dipped low over the lawn during the day, had gone to roost in the barn and pipistrelle bats had replaced them, flickering through the air, seemingly aimlessly.

I had reached the perimeter of the lawn, once again regretting the presence of the fence, a statement that made prisoners of us all, when I felt a gentle touch on my arm; I glanced down; a child's hands, hands bound with rope, the rope dripping water. For a moment I was incapable of movement, then I lifted my eyes to her face, a pretty girl, holding out her bound hands to me, her wide eyes, beseeching; behind her, her older sister, both dressed in wet rough spun cloth, aprons, their hair bundled up under white caps, small boots upon their feet. I feverishly tried to undo the knots, my own hands shaking with fear. The rope soaking wet, had swollen, making it difficult, but at last, almost desperately, I succeeded, as it grew darker. Nothing was said. In fact, I believe that I was incapable of speech.

They turned, embracing each other for a moment; watching them, my fear began to recede. I must have dropped to my knees with exhaustion and tears, for when I looked up, they were walking towards the cliff edge, holding hands, gradually fading through the fence. The taller one turned and glanced at me, smiling over her shoulder, before they were no more; then, there was just the sea breeze playing on my wet cheeks.

Strangely, I slept well that night, all the way through, as if a great weight had been removed from my mind. The house seemed warmer and lighter and the staff kinder and I began to settle down at last and write. I decided that in my intended novel I would give Anne and Hannah Kemp, a life. They would marry and have children, lead the life that had been taken so cruelly from them. I wasn't quite sure how, yet, but I had the feeling that they would guide me.

One morning, reading the local news, I saw that human bones had been found beneath the cliff; after much examination by experts, it was decided that they were the remains of Anne and Hannah Kemp. Weeks later I attended the burial service. I stood behind the small group, and as the Vicar came to the end of the service, bending and casting a handful of earth into the small grave, his white surplice, billowing out in the wind, for a moment, I thought I felt small hands in mine, one on each side. I would never be sure. But I liked to think that I had.

As I walked back to Wallbrooke Hall, I felt lighter in spirit than I had for some time. Anything was possible.

The Causeway.

It was on the second night that I heard it. Up until then I had slept moderately well; as well as one might in a strange bedroom. I had inadvertently been delayed up in Harrogate on a conference and instead of returning to London, an old school friend of mine who had been on the board, had invited me back to his house for a week. I knew that he lived near York but I had been completely unprepared for sheer grandeur of his abode. It was some ten miles out of York; An Elizabethan manor house with at least twelve bedrooms in a very attractive setting of thirty acres of deer park. I had known that he was exceedingly well off and had on occasion met his parents at school events. I had not seen him or been in contact with him for years and it had come very much as a pleasant surprise to find him at the conference.

I could have extended my stay in the hotel but it seemed churlish not to accept his offer and besides I was curious to learn how life had treated him since those days of our carefree youth. The house stood on a hill and it was fairly obvious that half of it no longer existed; one wing had been destroyed by fire in 1644, so that, in a way, it resembled a bird that was forever trying to take to the air; nevertheless, it was a masterpiece of Tudor brick and timber with four stately twisted brick chimneys reaching to the sky.

Inside it was dark but not at all unpleasant; light filtered through the small panes throwing shadows across the oak floors and bringing forth the subtle colours of tapestries and upholstery. My bedroom was large and sparse; my friend was adverse to unnecessary forms of ornamentation and comfort and the interior of the house must have remained untroubled by any alterations for many years; it was almost, I decided much as it had been in Elizabethan times, except for the plumbing and bathroom; even that was, I should think, Victorian. Yet I felt at ease, in another world that seemed to have retained a peace and tranquility, hard if not impossible to find elsewhere. Michael and his wife lived solely on the ground floor of this large house utilising the vast kitchen and the servants quarters leaving the rest of the house to the many guests that his corporate work entailed. At the time of my stay I was the only person in residence other than Michael and his wife. Michael was not exactly the perfect host, at least, not at this time and I detected an atmosphere between the two of them. For this reason I made myself as scarce as I could and tramped around the surrounding country during the weekend. We were due to return to Harrogate and complete our business towards the end of the following week but Michael was not the person that I had shared my youthful aspirations with in those years long past; people, of necessity, change which is easy to understand. I myself had changed; became more cautious and insular.

It was on the second night of my stay that I became aware of a strange disturbance which at first, half awake, I thought to be an argument; raised voices; perhaps it could be better termed as a disturbance; a change in the movement of air; in the very being of existence. It seemed sometimes during that night that I was in another age halfway between a dream and waking yet I was awake and conscious of something beyond my understanding. There were sounds and yet there was silence, as if when I concentrated they became non-existent; again, and again the sounds washed over me like waves in the sea unable to grasp. I must have slept at last for I became conscious of an unusual brightness in the room reflected on the low beamed ceiling. Snow had fallen overnight and lay thickly across the park. It occurred to me as I washed and dressed, that we might be cut off from our business in Harrogate for a few days, if not even longer for the clouds were heavy and low over the Howardian Hills and Sutton Bank.

After breakfast, during which neither Michael or his wife appeared, tired from the disturbances of the previous night, I decided to wrap up warm and get a breath of fresh air; there were several wellington boots in the lobby presumably for the use of guests and finding a pair that fitted me I set out into the deep snow. There were, very close to the front door, the tracks of what I thought was possibly a fox and later I was pleased to see the tracks of a hare, the long back feet; the bounding gait.

Then to my astonishment, close to the lake I found the snow churned up into great ruts some twenty feet across, a track which seemed to enter the lake and emerge from the far side; on closer inspection I could see the evidence of hundreds of boots and deep cart wheels as if an army had passed that way. I walked around the lake and it was much the same, a track; deep ruts that could only have been made by cart wheels and the undoubted evidence an army disappearing over the hill. I returned to the house my head in a whirl, eager to share my discovery.

'There was a causeway. Oh, I suppose in the 16th century,' Michael said over dinner that evening. 'The River Ouse flooded regularly in those days; in fact this was a floodplain and our house had been built on a hill; to get to Knaresborough on the old Roman Road was practically impossible for most of the winter so they built a causeway that joined the roman road higher up. After the Ouse was widened in the 17th century, one of my ancestors, Sis William Radcliffe, had it taken up and used the stones to build our magnificent mausoleum, in which he now resides.' He laughed. 'By the way there is no sign of a track as you described it. I walked over there this evening. The last fall of snow must have covered it up. We often get deer going down to the lake; sometimes quite a herd of them. They play the very devil with our young trees. You must have imagined it all- a trick of the light perhaps and you said you hadn't slept well.' With that, he dismissed it and turned to his wife who was regarding me curiously, her face pale.

'I've seen it, several times,' she said. 'The causeway. It stretches across the lake like a ribbon. Then just as you concentrate it dissembles, fades away.'

Michael laughed. 'Rubbish! Light off the water; it's an optical illusion like a mirage in the desert.'

'I know what I've seen.' she replied and for the rest of the meal was silent.

'How did the house come to be burnt, Michael?' I asked, to change the subject which was obviously one of deep contention.

'Oh, the Civil War. This was a royalist stronghold. The Parliamentarians set fire to it on their way to Marston Moor but luckily they didn't stay long and the servants fought all night to control it, after the Roundheads left.'

'Across the causeway?' I said quietly.

'Well, yes. It was the only way they could have gone.'

That night I stayed up, sitting in a chair by the window. There was a full moon; it was like fairyland, the lake itself liquid silver the trees casting dark shadows on the pristine white blanket of snow; the moon was over the far end of the lake creating a path of shimmering silver; one could almost imagine a causeway across it. The experience I had felt the night before was not repeated. The snow lay undisturbed, except for a lone fox loping, head close to the ground.

I firmly believe to this day, that an army had passed that way that night, a parliamentarian army on its way to Marston Moor where it defeated the Royalists and held the town of Knaresborough to siege. On the way it set fire to the hall. The strange noises I had heard were snatches of a desperate encounter from the past; movement of air and smoke; a tiny break in the thick curtain that divides this life from other lives

The Telephone Exchange

They told me it was on the right at the top of the hill but a mist had come down in the last hour and I was having difficulty finding it.

There had been very few lights showing as I had made my way out of the village of Havodglas. Most of it was now deserted and left to the sheep to roam in amongst the ruins of cottages, the roofs and walls gradually returning to nature as the winter storms and the lack of employment took their toll. The inhabitants, those that had not died and lay buried in the small churchyard, after years of toil in the slate mine, had left for the nearby city.

My wife had laughed when I suggested following up the advert 'Telephone Exchange for sale.' It was true, she said, that we were seeking somewhere quiet, where we could pursue our respective creative paths, in a beautiful part of the world. But a telephone exchange! She reminded me how I had nearly bought a railway signal box near Exeter until I discovered the trains passed every half hour.

Nevertheless I had set out one winters day, from Bristol, and crossed the bridge into that land of myth and legend, the marches that lay between Wales and England, that in-between world that no-one can quite take for granted.

The attraction to the Telephone Exchange was not just a whim on my part. I had started my working life in a telephone exchange working for the then GPO, straight from school, employed in the change from manual to automatic, taking out the rows of mahogany desks with all the plugs and leads, where rows of girls had once sat and laughed and chatted as they linked up distant voices across the ether and gradually replacing them with metal frames and thick coils of wire that sent signals to clacking machinery seeking out the dialed numbers.

I had thought it was a sad time. There seemed to me so much more beauty in those desks and the young and vibrant girls that had performed those feats of interaction, than these cold metal frames and clacking machinery.

It appeared that the Havodglas Telephone Exchange had been empty for some years and had preceded the time of automation. It had been built in the 1930s when Havodglas was a thriving town and with many links to the nearby habitations and the daughters of the miners, were a natural given workforce for the aspiration of the then thriving telecommunication side of the GPO. It was almost impossible to imagine what it must have been like in that thriving community all those years ago before modernity had ironed it flat leaving it impoverished in its wake.

It was, with these thoughts in my mind that suddenly I saw it looming out of the mist, a great oblong building, with those large Georgian windows that I remembered so well, in other exchanges that I had known.

I had meant to arrive before the light had faded but I had been held up on the bridge for some time by a lorry which had crossed the barrier and had hung over the river Seven precariously for two hours while we filed past at a maddingly slow rate, now and then stopping altogether. The estate agent in Monmouth had gaily informed me that there were some lights working, enough probably to get a fair idea of the state of the fabric of the building which they said was in surprisingly good condition. I had the good sense to bring a powerful torch, for in my experience nothing went exactly to plan.

My wife had asked if was not a little scared but I had joked that any attractive telephone girls would be welcomed with open arms as far as I was concerned. The door gave way at a push and I had no need to use the heavy key. I felt for the light switch and a bare bulb flickered into life casting heavy shadows on the walls and the stairs that led upwards into the darkness. Double doors led into what would have been, in those days when the village was at its height, the post office counter, with probably a small sorting office at the rear.

The building would have been a hive of activity with postman and girl telephonists. Now it was dark and deserted. Curious for a moment, I listened for those sounds of the past, which surely must be ingrained in the very fabric of the building. Nothing; just the wind howling through a broken window pane.

To my surprise the post office was intact and had not been touched in anyway. There had been talk of a museum before local funds ran out. I could see how it could easily could be converted into living quarters and good use made of the furnishings, which were of the highest quality.

A quick look at the upstairs and then I would make my way home to a warm fire and dinner. I had no wish to stay longer. I was by no means certain that the locality was suitable, although the building was just what I expected.

As I neared the top of the stairs the light flickered and left me in sudden darkness. Congratulating myself on the foresight to bring a torch, I switched it on and opened the double doors, playing the beam around the huge room. To my utter astonishment all the switchboards were still in place. A row of twenty, I counted as I walked around, my mind in a whirl. The plugs all neatly in place as if waiting for the next call. It must have been fifty years since automation had swept these much-loved art deco cabinets away with their revolving seats. Strangely, no mention had been made of them in the estate agents particulars.

It was at this moment I dropped my torch. Try as I might in the resulting darkness I could not locate it and a feeling of panic overtook me. Whether it was the shock of seeing the switchboards, as if I had been transported back fifty years or so, or something else. An innate fear of the dark and the unknown.

I reached out hoping to guide myself back to the door, the stairs and out where I could breathe easier again and regain my composure. Something brushed against my hand, material, a warmth; a person. Then I heard laughter, as if from a long way away. Female voices; perfume; a soft hand on my arm; a whispering my ear. The sound of laughter grew louder.

Shaking, I dropped to my knees crawling towards the faint light from the doors, my heart thumping, reaching the stairs and the outside.

As I gained the safety of my car I looked back. The upper floor was ablaze with lights.

'So how was it?' My wife asked, laughing, as we sat down to dinner. 'Did you meet any pretty young telephonists?'

It was at this moment that I knew that I could never talk to her about it. I remembered the gentle touch on my arm the soft voice in my ear. It was a world that I would gladly return to if it was possible. That world when people mattered and lives were simpler and innocent, or is that just a fantasy that I harbour. I like to think it true.

Printed in Great Britain
by Amazon